Dear Parent:

Congratulations! Your child is taking the first steps on an exciting journey. The destination? Independent reading!

STEP INTO READING® will help your child get there. The pro␣ offers books at five levels that accompany children from their first attempts at reading to reading success. Each step includes fun stories, fiction and nonfiction, and colorful art. There are also Step into Reading Sticker Books, Step into Reading Math Readers, and Step into Reading Phonics Readers— a complete literacy program with something to interest every child.

Learning to Read, Step by Step!

Ready to Read   Preschool–Kindergarten
• **big type and easy words** • **rhyme and rhythm** • **picture clues**
For children who know the alphabet and are eager to begin reading.

Reading with Help   Preschool–Grade 1
• **basic vocabulary** • **short sentences** • **simple stories**
For children who recognize familiar words and sound out new words with help.

Reading on Your Own   Grades 1–3
• **engaging characters** • **easy-to-follow plots** • **popular topics**
For children who are ready to read on their own.

Reading Paragraphs   Grades 2–3
• **challenging vocabulary** • **short paragraphs** • **exciting stories**
For newly independent readers who read simple sentences with confidence.

Ready for Chapters   Grades 2–4
• **chapters** • **longer paragraphs** • **full-color art**
For children who want to take the plunge into chapter books but still like colorful pictures.

STEP INTO READING® is designed to give every child a successful reading experience. The grade levels are only guides. Children can progress through the steps at their own speed, developing confidence in their reading, no matter what their grade.

Remember, a lifetime love of reading starts with a single step!

www.randomhouse.com/kids
www.barbie.com
Educators and librarians, for a variety of teaching tools visit us at
www.randomhouse.com/teachers

Library of Congress Cataloging-in-Publication Data
Pugliano-Martin, Carol.
Barbie : a day at the fair / by Carol Pugliano-Martin ; illustrated by S.I. International.
   p.   cm. — (Step into reading. Step 2 book)
SUMMARY: Barbie and Kelly go to the fair and even ride the Ferris wheel.
ISBN 0-375-82368-9 (trade) — ISBN 0-375-92368-3 (lib. bdg.)
[1. Fairs—Fiction. 2. Ferris wheels—Fiction. 3. Dolls—Fiction.] I. S.I. International (Firm), ill.
II. Title. III. Series.
PZ7.P148 Bar 2003 [E]—dc21 2002010237

Printed in the United States of America 10 9 8 7 6 5 4 3 2

STEP INTO READING®

STEP 2

Barbie
A Day at the Fair

By Carol Pugliano-Martin
Illustrated by S.I. International

Random House New York

It was a big day!
Barbie was
already dressed.
But Kelly was
still in bed.

"Time to get up!"
said Barbie.
"We are going
to the fair!"

Kelly jumped out of bed.

"Oh, boy!" she said.

"I will ride

the Ferris wheel

all by myself!"

Barbie helped Kelly
get dressed.
"The Ferris wheel
is pretty big," she said.
"Maybe I should
ride it with you."

"No, thank you,"
said Kelly.
"I can ride by myself."

When they got
to the fair,
Kelly ran to
the Ferris wheel.

She looked up, up, up
at the Ferris wheel.
It was very big.
And *very* tall!

"Are you ready to ride
the Ferris wheel?"
asked Barbie.
"Not yet," said Kelly.

Kelly and Barbie
saw a lady
making cotton candy.
They each had a
fluffy pink cone.

"Are you ready to ride
the Ferris wheel?"
asked Barbie.
"Not yet," said Kelly.

Kelly and Barbie
went inside
the animal tent.
Kelly oinked at a pig.

She petted a cow.

She even fed hay

to a goat.

18

They went back outside.
"Are you ready to ride
the Ferris wheel?"
asked Barbie.
"Not yet," said Kelly.

Kelly went
on a pony ride.
She waved to Barbie.

"Are you ready to ride
the Ferris wheel now?"
asked Barbie.

"Not yet," said Kelly.

Kelly and Barbie watched
the Ferris wheel
go around and around.
The children
riding on it
were smiling.

"Kelly, do you want
me to ride with you?"
asked Barbie.
"Yes!" said Kelly.

She and Barbie got onto
the Ferris wheel.

At first,
Kelly felt afraid.
She shut her eyes.
Barbie held her close.
They went up, up, up.

At the top,
Kelly opened her eyes.
She had never been
so high up before!
She could see
the whole fair.
"Wow!" said Kelly.
"This is fun!"

The Ferris wheel
went down, down, down.
Soon the ride was over.
"I want to ride again!"
said Kelly.

And that is just what
Barbie and Kelly did.